llama llama red pajama

written and illustrated by

Anna Dewdney

SCHOLASTIC INC.

New York Toronto London Auckland Sydney
Mexico City New Delhi Hong Kong Buenos Aires

ISBN-13: 978-0-439-90665-4
ISBN-10: 0-439-90665-2

30 29 28 27 26 25   13 14 15/0

Printed in the U.S.A.   40

First Scholastic printing, October 2006

Set in Quorum
Designed by Kelley McIntyre

For my own little llamas,

with thanks to Tracy, Denise, and Deborah.

Llama llama
red pajama
reads a story
with his mama.

Mama kisses
baby's hair.
Mama Llama
goes downstairs.

Llama llama
red pajama
feels **alone**
without his mama.

Baby Llama wants a drink.

Mama's at the kitchen sink.

Llama llama
red pajama
calls down to
his llama mama.

Mama says
she'll be up soon.

Baby Llama
hums a tune.

Llama llama
red pajama
waiting waiting
for his mama.

Mama isn't
coming yet.
Baby Llama
starts to **fret.**

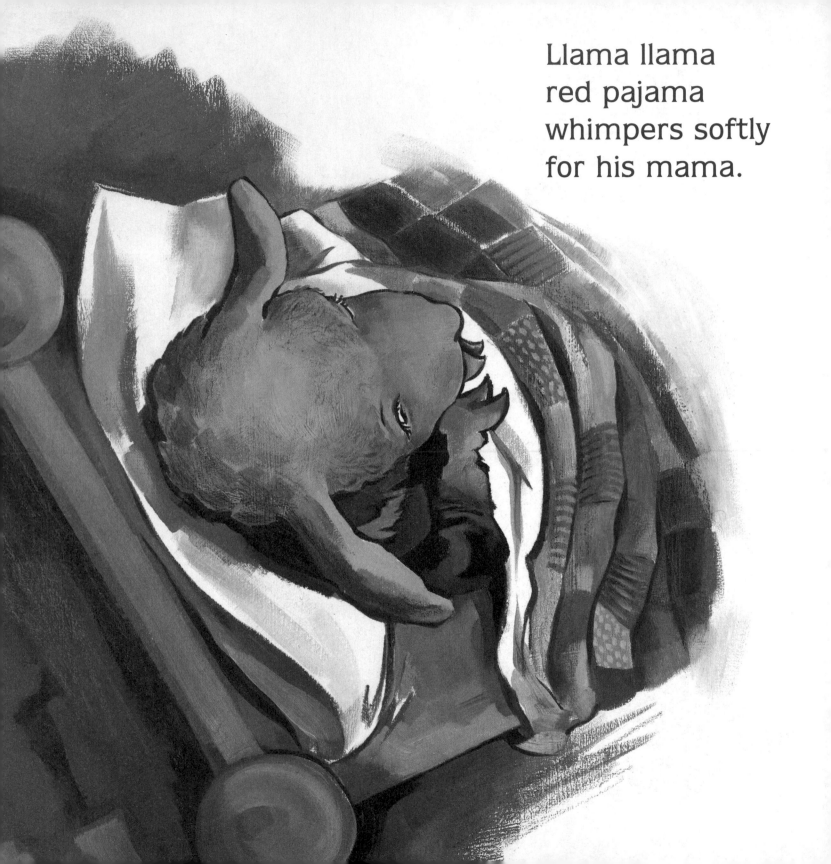

Llama llama
red pajama
whimpers softly
for his mama.

Mama Llama
hears the phone.

Baby Llama
starts to **moan**. . . . .

Llama llama
red pajama
listens, quiet,
for his mama.

What is Mama Llama doing?

Baby Llama
starts **boo hoo-ing.**

Llama llama
red pajama
hollers loudly
for his mama.

Baby Llama
stomps and **pouts.**

Baby Llama
jumps and **shouts.**

Llama llama
red pajama
in the dark
without his mama.
Eyes wide open,
covers drawn . . .
What if Mama Llama's **GONE?**

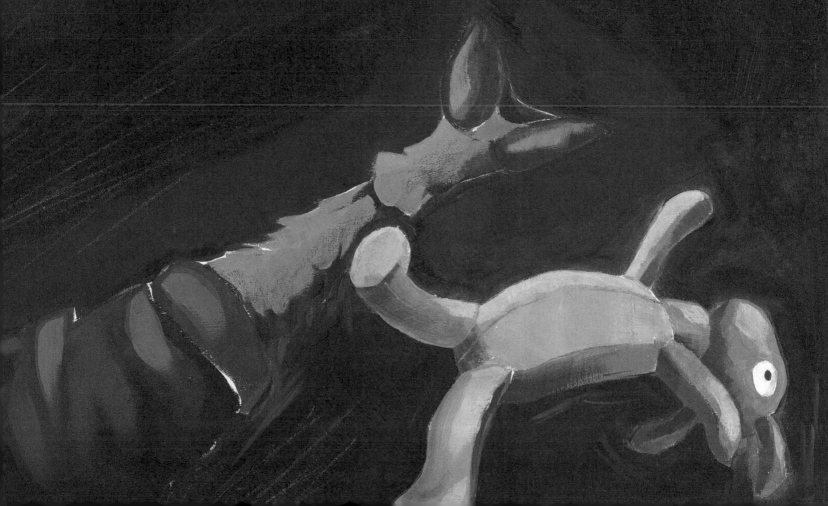

Llama llama
red pajama
weeping, wailing
for his mama.
Will his mama ever come?
Mama Llama, **RUN RUN RUN!**

Baby Llama,
what a **tizzy!**
Sometimes Mama's
very busy.

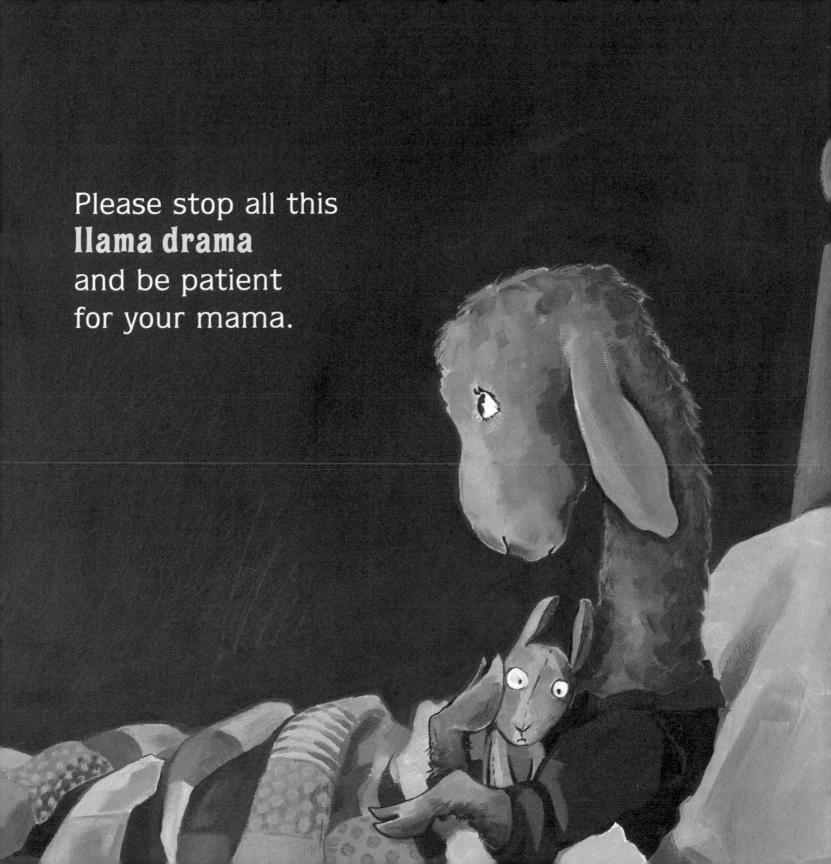

Please stop all this
llama drama
and be patient
for your mama.

Little Llama,
don't you know,
Mama Llama
loves you so?

Mama Llama's
always near,
even if she's
not right **here.**

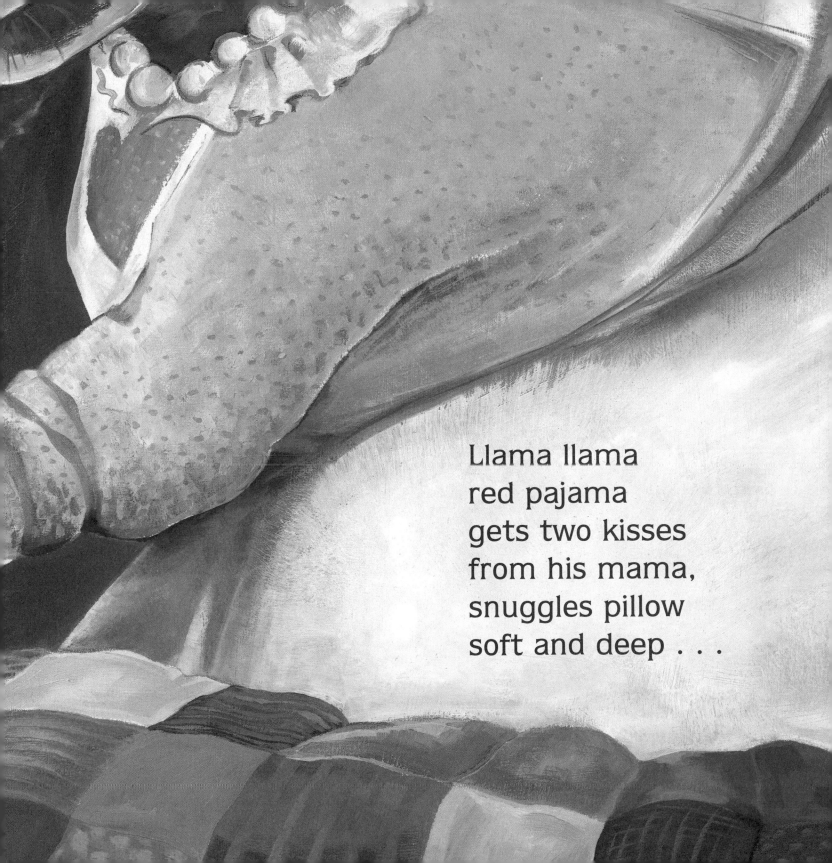

Llama llama
red pajama
gets two kisses
from his mama,
snuggles pillow
soft and deep . . .

Baby Llama
goes to **sleep.**